BRIMSTONE
BY SHIRVANIAN

A TOM DOHERTY ASSOCIATES BOOK
NEW YORK

This is a work of fiction. All the characters and events portrayed in this book are fictitious, and any resemblance to real people or events is purely coincidental.

BRIMSTONE #2

Copyright © 1983, 1988 by King Features Syndicate

All rights reserved, including the right to reproduce this book or portions thereof in any form.

A TOR Book
Published by Tom Doherty Associates, Inc.
49 West 24 Street
New York, NY 10010

ISBN: 0-812-56275-5   Can. ISBN: 0-812-56276-3

First edition: December 1988

Printed in the United States of America

0 9 8 7 6 5 4 3 2 1

KELLY'S GAS
© 1981 King Features Syndicate, Inc. World rights reserved.
10/7
ZZZ
BRIMSTONE
HEE HEE HOO HOO
BRIM

TOO HOT!
© 1981 King Features Syndicate, Inc. World rights reserved.
BRIMSTONE
9/28
BRIM

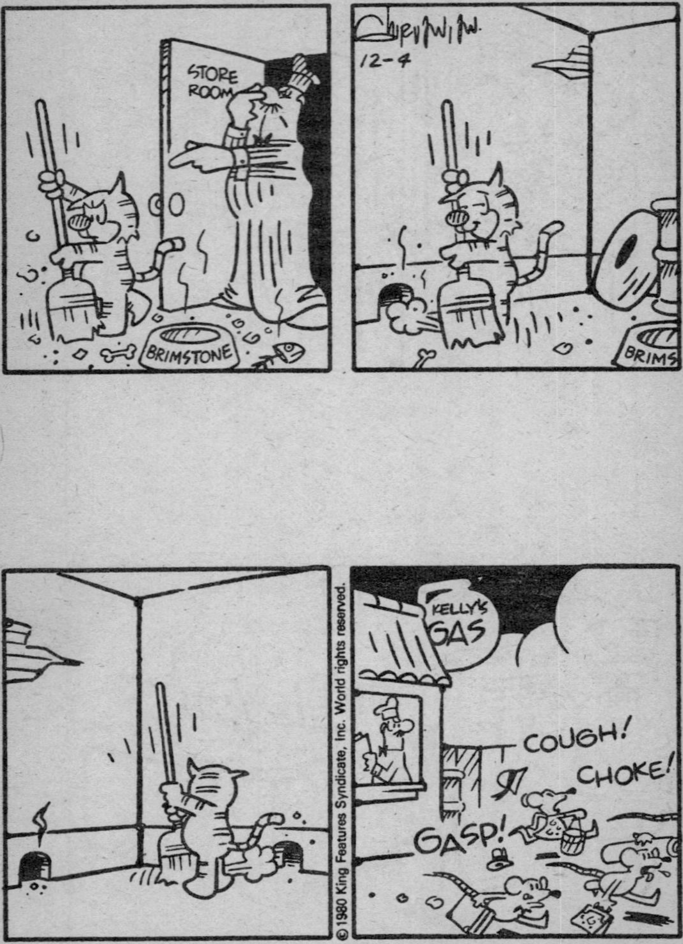
STORE ROOM
BRIMSTONE
12-4
BRIMS
KELLY'S GAS
COUGH!
CHOKE!
GASP!

BRIMSTONE
SOAK 'N CLEAN
BRIMSTONE
SOAK 'N CLEAN
BRIMSTONE
SOAK 'N CLEAN
BRIMSTONE
12-6

KELLY'S GAS
BRIMSTONE
PARTS DEPT.
PARTS DEPT.
OIL FILTER
PARTS DEPT.
12-16
CHICKEN WINGS

KELLY'S GAS
BRIMSTONE
VA-VA-VA VOOM!
PLAY GUY
HUBBA HUBBA!
© 1980 King Features Syndicate, Inc. World rights reserved.
12-11

PEANUT BUTTER AND JELLY!
LIVER LUMPS
BRIMSTONE
BRIMSTONE

12-13
©1990 King Features Syndicate, Inc. World rights reserved.
BR

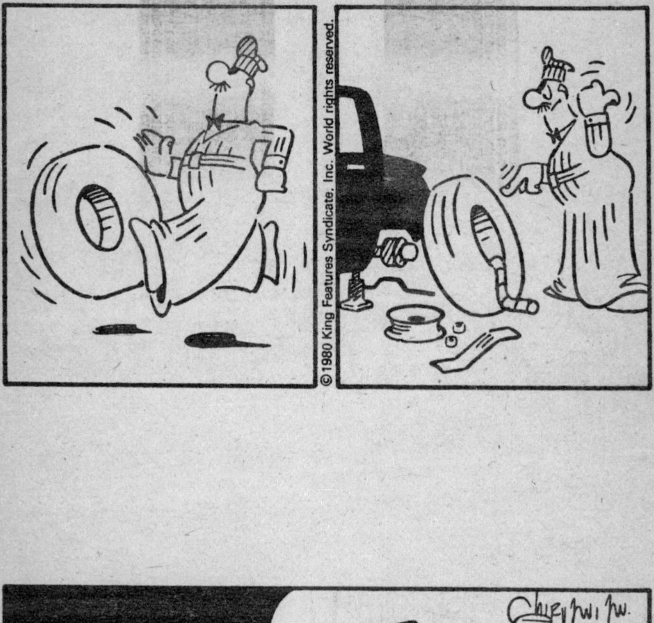
KELLY'S GAS
BRIMSTONE
12-3

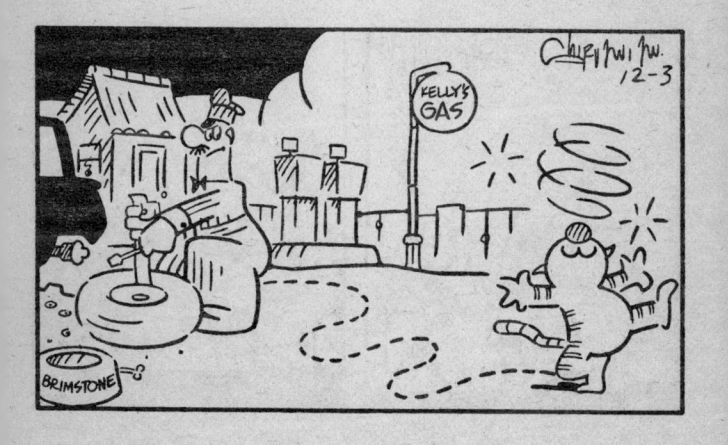

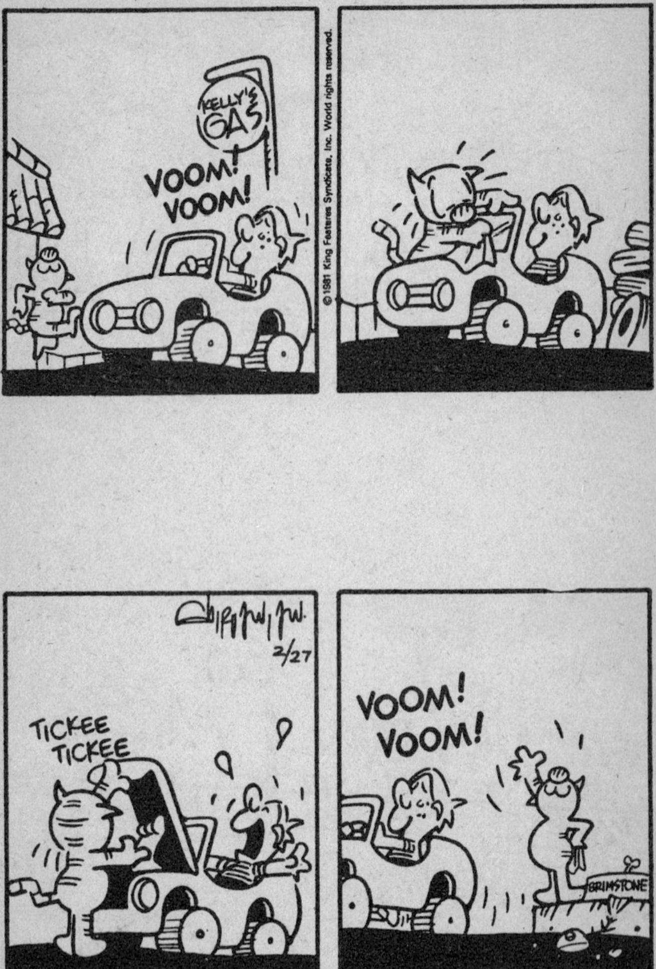
KELLY'S GAS
VOOM! VOOM!
2/27
TICKEE TICKEE
VOOM! VOOM!
BRIMSTONE

© 1981 King Features Syndicate, Inc. World rights reserved.
SNIFF!
TV SOAP OPERAS TODAY
SNIFF!
BRIMSTONE

3/23
TV SOAP OPERAS TODAY
SNIFF!
BRIMSTONE

© 1981 King Features Syndicate, Inc. World rights reserved.
1–6
Z
Z
Z
BURP!
Z
Z

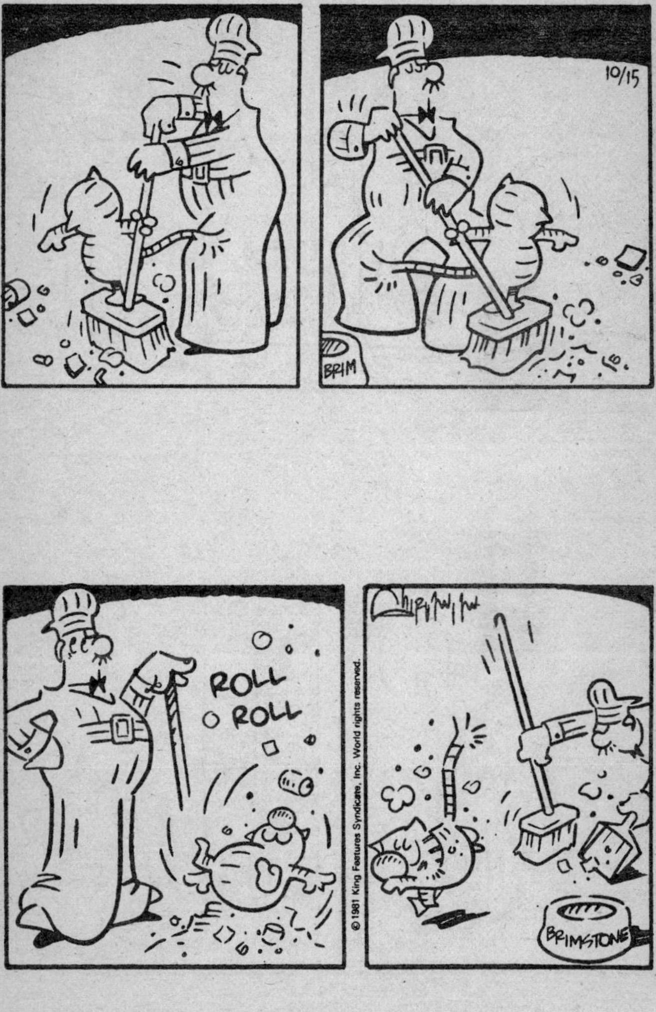
10/15
BRIM
ROLL
ROLL
BRIMSTONE

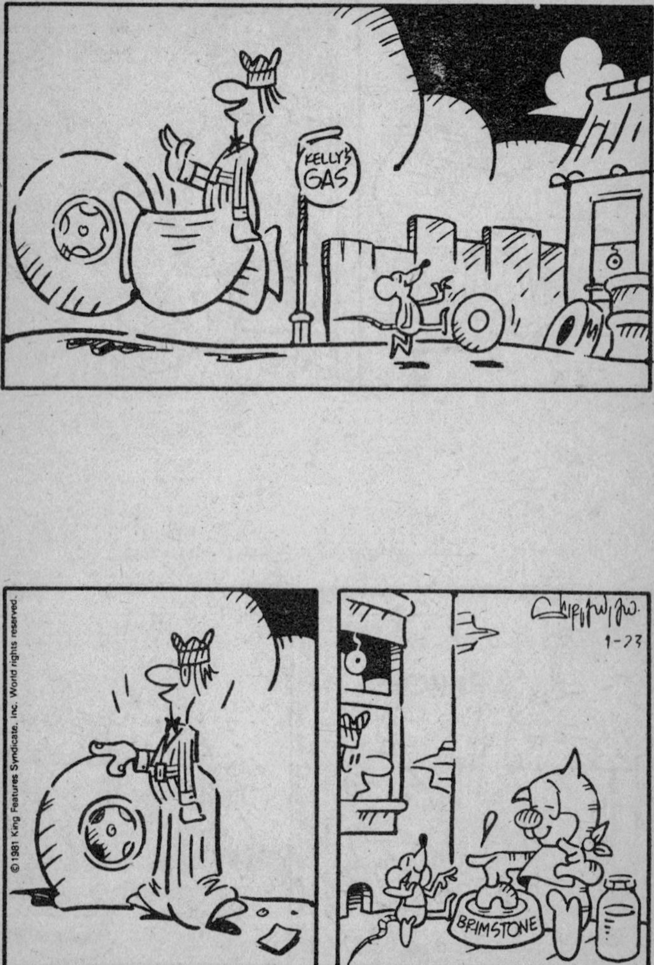
KELLY'S
GAS
1-23
BRIMSTONE

THIS END UP
BRIM
© 1981 King Features Syndicate, Inc. World rights reserved.
THIS END UP
10/31
THIS END UP
BRIMSTONE
THIS END UP

BRIMSTONE
BRIMSTONE'S DIET
1. NO SWEETS
2. AVOID STARCHES
3. DRINK PLENTY OF WATER
1-30
BRIMSTONE
BRIMSTONE
BRIMSTONE
© 1981 King Features Syndicate, Inc. World rights reserved.

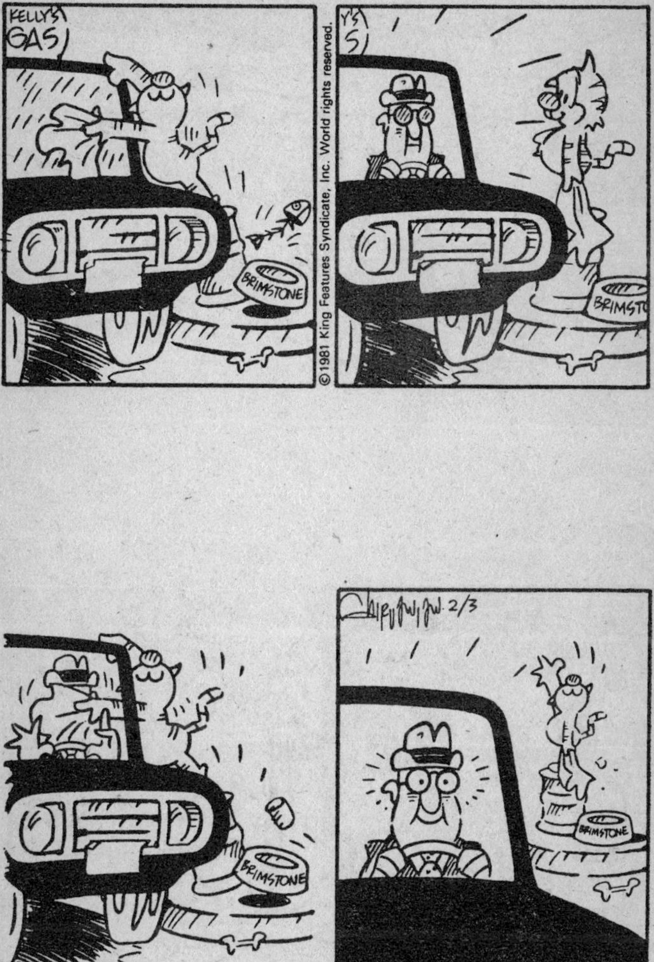
KELLY'S
GAS
BRIMSTONE
©1981 King Features Syndicate, Inc. World rights reserved.
BRIMSTONE
BRIMSTONE
2/3

REPAIRS
ESTIMATE
$74.55
PLUS TAX
REPAIRS
FREE ESTIMATES

REPAIRS
Ernie's
FISH
MARKET
WE DELIVER
OR $64.55
PLUS
BRIMSTONE
1-9

KELLY'S GAS
BRIMSTONE
©1981 King Features Syndicate, Inc. World rights reserved.
WASH ROOM
BRIMS
WASH ROOM
1-8
PULL DOWN

GRIMM'S FAIRY TALES
BRIMSTONE
© 1981 King Features Syndicate, Inc. World rights reserved
STORE ROOM
BRIMSTONE
1–7
BRIMSTONE

BRIMSTONE
POUNCE!
6/16
©1981 King Features Syndicate, Inc. World rights reserved.

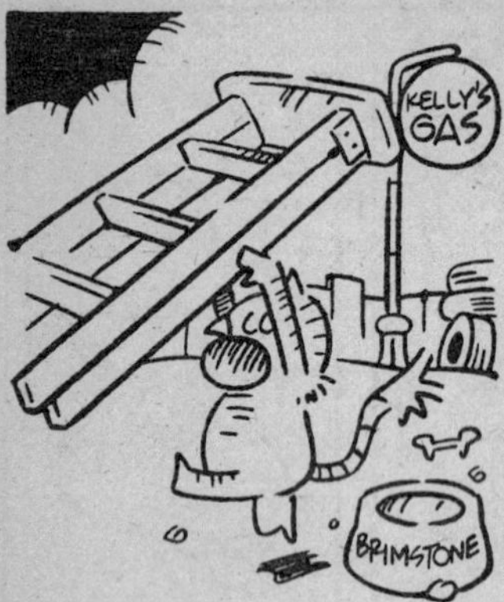
KELLY'S GAS
BRIMSTONE

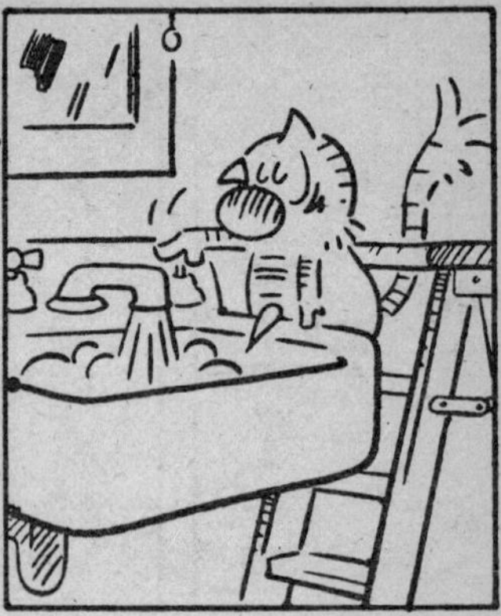

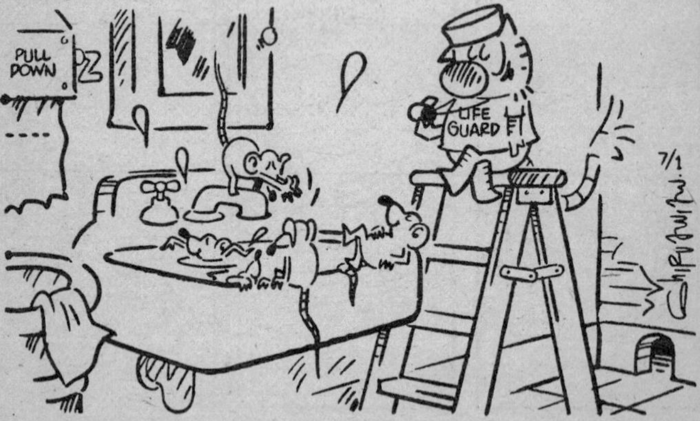
PULL DOWN
LIFE GUARD
7/1

DAILY
ACTRESS VISITS CITY
FIFI LATOUR
8/3

PURRRR!
KELLY'S GAS
MOTOR OIL
BRIMSTONE
FIFI

BRIMSTONE
WHAT AN UGLY DISH
BRIMSTONE
CAT FOOD
BRIMSTONE
I LOVE MY UGLY DISH!
8/24
BRIMSTONE

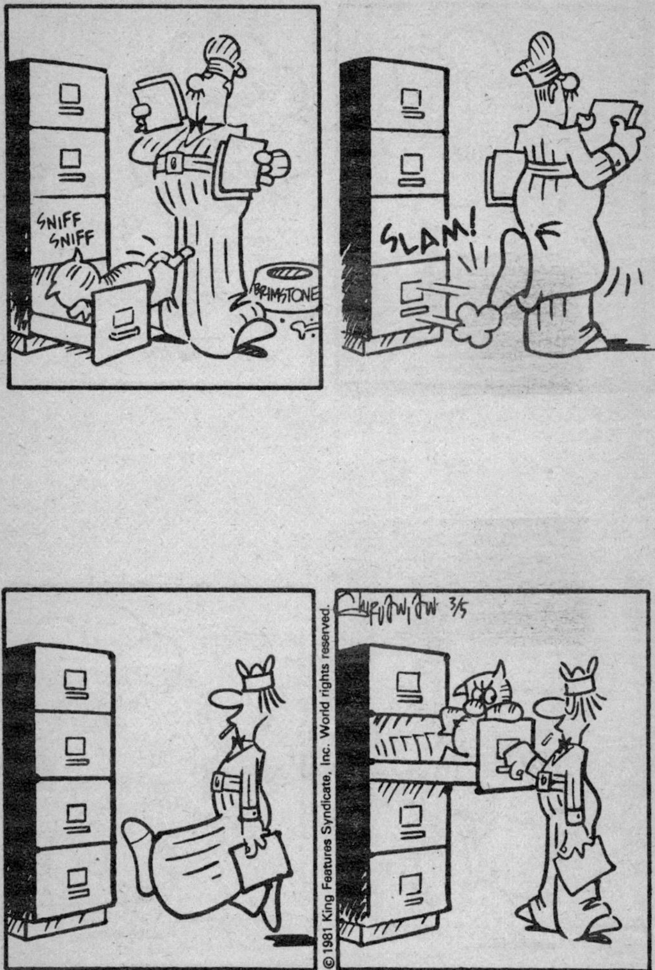
SNIFF
SNIFF
BRIMSTONE
SLAM!

AH! THE SMELL OF CRISP, COOL AIR!
10-21
THE FRAGRANCE OF TANGY PINE NEEDLES!
Z Z Z
BRIMSTONE
© 1980 King Features Syndicate, Inc. World rights reserved.
THE SCENT OF AUTUMN LEAVES!

KELLY'S GAS
VOOM VOOM!
SODA
COIN
GLUG!
DON'T DRINK AND DRIVE
MOTOR OIL
BRIMS
ZZZZZ
ZZZZ
MOTOR OIL
BRIMSTONE

BUSINESS-MAN ON HIS WAY TO HIS OFFICE
9/11
SNIFF SNIFF
WITH SALAMI ON RYE FOR HIS LUNCH!
©1981 King Features Syndicate, Inc. World rights reserved.

BRIMSTONE
TONE
© 1981 King Features Syndicate, Inc. World rights reserved.

4/25

RUFF RUFF RUFF RUFF!
KELLY'S GAS
BRIMSTONE
YIP YIP YIP?
YIP YIP YIP!
YIP YIP YIP!
BRIMSTONE

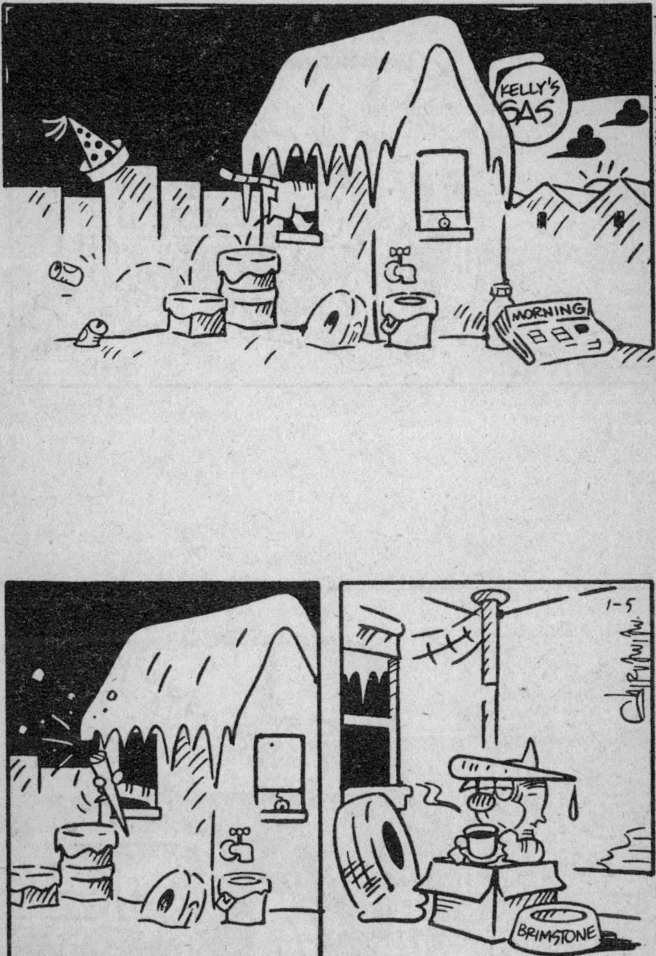

KELLY'S GAS
MORNING
1-5
BRIMSTONE

KELLY'S GAS
BRIMSTONE
©1981 King Features Syndicate, Inc. World rights reserved.

ONE
1-22

BAR
EXIT
BOOT!
© 1981 King Features Syndicate, Inc. World rights reserved.
1-21
BOOT!
KELLY'S
GAS

BRIMSTONE'S NEW YEAR'S RESOLUTIONS
NO. 1—
BRIMSTONE
SNAP!
BRIMSTONE
© 1980 King Features Syndicate, Inc. World rights reserved.
BRIMSTONE
N N N N N
1-1
BRIMSTONE

ROYAL ARMS
NOW RENTING
NO PETS
ROYAL ARMS
NOW RENTING
NO PETS

8/25
ROYAL ARMS UNFAIR TO PETS
ROYAL ARMS NOT NICE
END DISCRIMINATION AT ROYAL ARMS

8/29

© 1981 King Features Syndicate, Inc. World rights reserved.
KISS!
BRIMSTONE

9/2
SWISH!

9/4

SAVE WATER
SAVE WATER
©1981 King Features Syndicate, Inc. World rights reserved.
9/5

SAVE WATER
GARGLE WITH A FRIEND

BRIMSTONE

LICK!
LICK!
LICK!
BRIMSTONE
I HATE BATH NIGHT!
I HATE BATH NIGHT!
BRIMSTONE
1-31

SODA
COIN
BOOST!
BRIMSTONE
OOF!
PUSH!
SHOVE!
BRIM
PLUNK!
©1981 King Features Syndicate, Inc. World rights reserved.
POP!
9/8
COIN RETURN
PLOP!

CASINO
© 1981 King Features Syndicate, Inc. World rights reserved.
9/10

Z
Z
Z
LEAP!
© 1981 King Features Syndicate, Inc. World rights reserved.
BOUNCE!
9/12
Z
Z
THAT'S FUNNY! THERE USED TO BE A LAP THERE!
BRIMSTONE

CAT FOOD
BRIMSTONE
KELLY'S GAS
LEAP!
ZOOM!
SCREECH!
CAT FOOD
HO HUM!
BRIMSTONE
© 1981 King Features Syndicate, Inc. World rights reserved.
9/15

9/16

Z Z Z
BRIMSTONE
Z Z Z Z
BRIMSTONE
Z Z Z
BRIMSTONE
Z Z Z
BRIMSTONE
9/18

SNIFF
SNIFF
BRIMSTONE
BONK!
© 1981 King Features Syndicate, Inc. World rights reserved.
9/19
SMUMPH!
SMACK!
YUM!

LEAP!
DIAL
DIAL
© 1981 King Features Syndicate, Inc. World rights reserved.
GASP!
PANT!
PANT!
BRIMSTONE
9/22
TOM'S
PIZZA
FREE
DELIVERY

POOR THING!
BRI
©1981 King Features Syndicate, Inc. World rights reserved.
SHE NEEDS ALL THE LOVE AND SYMPATHY SHE CAN GET
PURRRR
BRIMSTONE

HER CAR'S IN INTENSIVE CARE
OIL
KELLY'S GAS
9/23
BRIM

THE POWER OF THE MIND
BRIMSTONE
BRIMSTONE
BRIMSTONE
9/24
© 1981 King Features Syndicate, Inc. World rights reserved.
CAT FOOD
ACTUALLY, I WAS CONCENTRATING ON ROAST TURKEY!
BRIMSTONE

© 1981 King Features Syndicate, Inc. World rights reserved.
ROLL! ROLL! ROLL!
9/26

HAPPY BIRTHDAY, KELLY!
CLINK
© 1981 King Features Syndicate, Inc. World rights reserved.
CLINK!
BRIMSTONE
CLINK!
BRIMSTONE
1-28
GULP!
GULP!
GULP!
BRIMSTONE

©1981 King Features Syndicate, Inc. World rights reserved.
BRIMSTONE
4/8
TONE

©1981 King Features Syndicate, Inc. World rights reserved.
10/12
I WAS CHEERING FOR THEM!
PANT PANT

7/24

ASSORTED CHEESES AND JAMS FOR GRANDMA!
GRANDMA
BRIMSTONE
12/23

MUMPH! SMACK!
I'M SURE GRANDMA WILL BE JUST AS PLEASED WITH A FAT PUSSYCAT!

SOAP
SOAP
SOAP
© 1980 King Features Syndicate, Inc. World rights reserved.
CHECK OUT
GARDEN SUPPLY
DIRT
DIRT
DIRT
LIME
LIME
LIME
LIME
POTTING SOIL
11-20

© 1981 King Features Syndicate, Inc. World rights reserved.
2/18
BRIMSTONE
SPORTS
BIG GAME ON TV

PTOO!
BRIMSTONE

M-M-M!
SMACK!
BRIMSTONE
CHICKEN GIZZARDS?
LIVER LUMPS?
FISH HEADS?
BRIMSTONE!
©1980 King Features Syndicate, Inc. World rights reserved.
12-27

BRIMSTO
DAILY
CAT INHERITS MILLION DOLLARS
BILL
BILL

2/2
KELLY BANK BOOK

DAILY
CAT GOES TO POOR-HOUSE
BRIMSTONE
BRIMSTONE

MILK BATHS ARE REFRESHING
©1981 King Features Syndicate, Inc. World rights reserved.

—BUT DANGEROUS!
BRIMSTONE

YAWN
BRIMSTONE
©1981 King Features Syndicate, Inc. World rights reserved.
CLICK!
BRIMSTONE
BONK!
7/17
CLICK
!!!
BRIMSTONE

KELLY'S
GAS
KELLY'S
GAS
© 1980 King Features Syndicate, Inc. World rights reserved.
11-15
BRIMSTONE

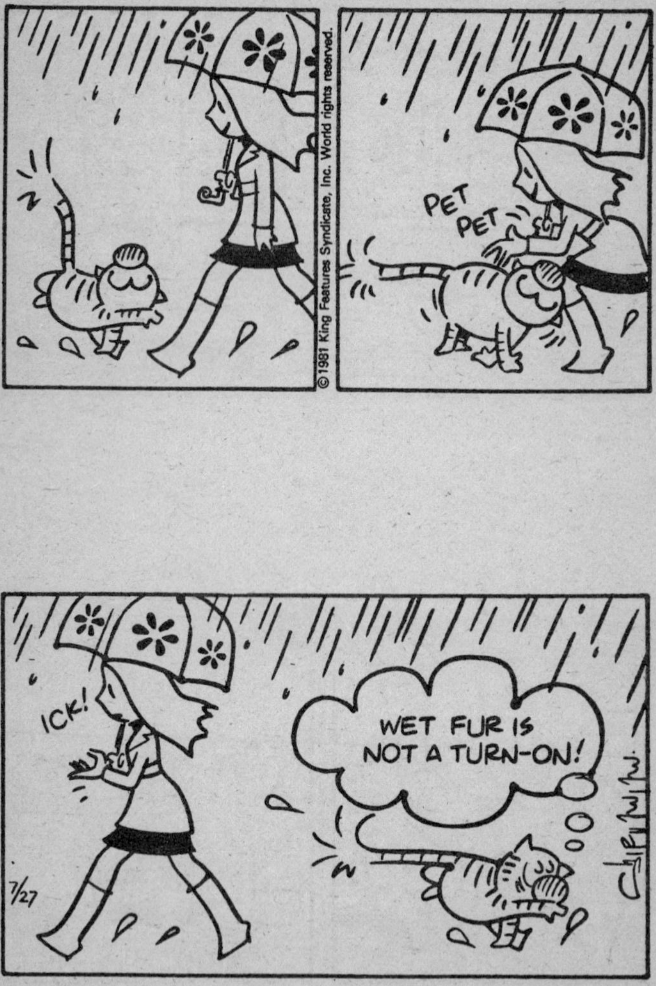
PET
PET
ICK!
WET FUR IS NOT A TURN-ON!
7/27

Z Z Z Z
BRIMSTONE
CRASH!
RUMBLE!
BOOM!
BRIMSTONE
©1981 King Features Syndicate, Inc. World rights reserved.
2/14
BRIMSTONE
THE BRIMSTONE ADVISER
IN CASE OF EARTHQUAKE MAKE SURE YOUR MILK DISH IS EMPTY
BRIMSTONE

KELLY'S GAS
REGULAR
SUPER
UNLEADED
MOTOR OIL
BRIMSTONE
8/19
KELLY'S GAS
SUPER
UNLEADED
UNLOVED
BRIMSTONE

SLIP!
HOW DID I GET HERE?
WHO CARES?!
8/17
© 1981 King Features Syndicate, Inc. World rights reserved.

©1981 King Features Syndicate, Inc. World rights reserved.
2/19
PECK!

PECK PECK!
PECK PECK!
PECK PECK PECK!
PECK!

TSK! TSK!

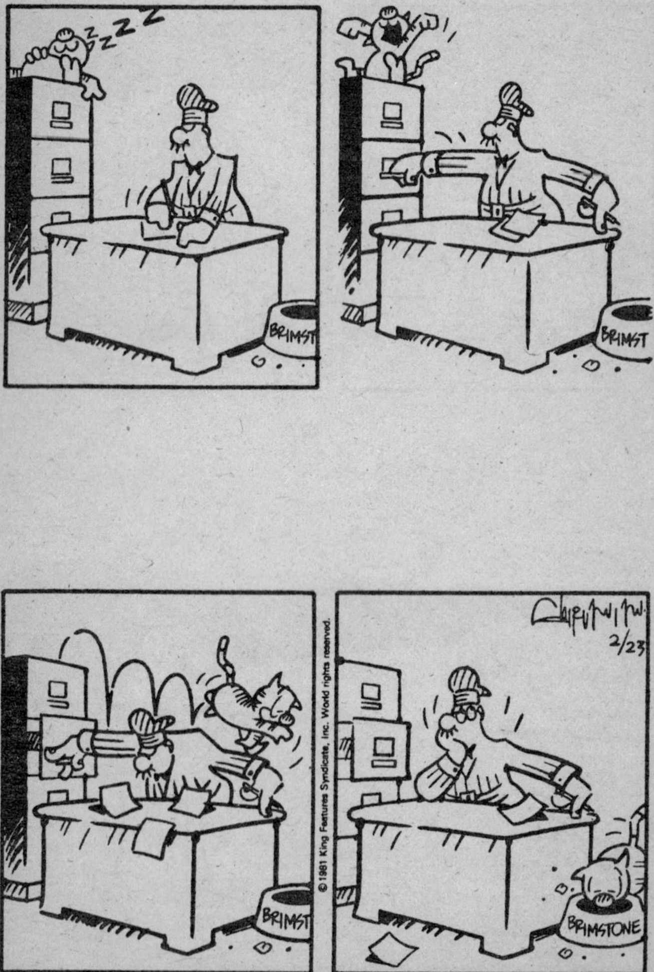
BRIMST
BRIMST
BRIMST
BRIMSTONE
2/23

©1981 King Features Syndicate, Inc. World rights reserved.
2/24

KELLY'S GAS
BRIMS
GAS
MOTOR OIL
BRIMS
GAS
MOTOR OIL
BRIMSTONE
2/25

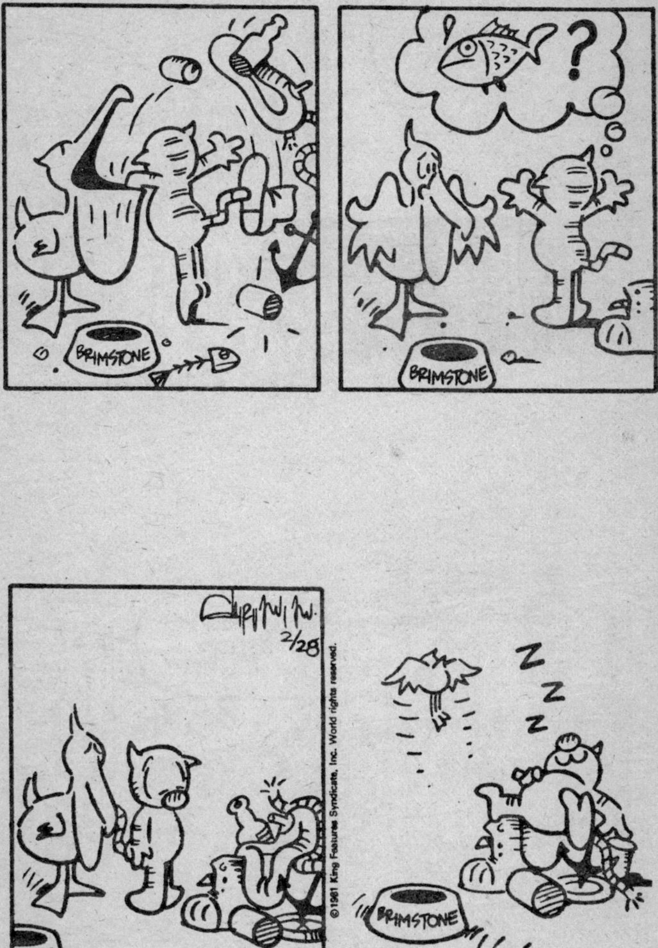
BRIMSTONE
?
BRIMSTONE
2/28
STONE
Z Z Z
BRIMSTONE

SAUTÉED KIDNEYS—
HIS FAVORITE!
PURRRRR
BRIMS
© 1981 King Features Syndicate, Inc. World rights reserved.
BONK!
PURRRR
BRIMSTONE

I JUST HOPE THEY'RE
READY BEFORE
HE KILLS HIMSELF!
KELLY'S
GAS
BONK!
PURRR
BRIMSTONE
3/2

Z Z Z Z Z
BRIMSTONE
©1981 King Features Syndicate, Inc. World rights reserved.
eee!!!
BRIMSTONE
eee!!!

BRIMSTONE
BRIMSTONE
3/7
© 1981 King Features Syndicate, Inc. World rights reserved.
KELLY'S GAS

SMACK!
LIVER LUMPS
BRIMSTONE
BRIMSTONE
BRIMSTONE
© 1980 King Features Syndicate, Inc. World rights reserved.
12-12
BRIMSTONE

BED-TIME TALES
BRIMSTONE
©1980 King Features Syndicate, Inc. World rights reserved.
Z Z Z
BRIMSTONE
Z Z Z Z Z Z
BRIMSTONE
12-26

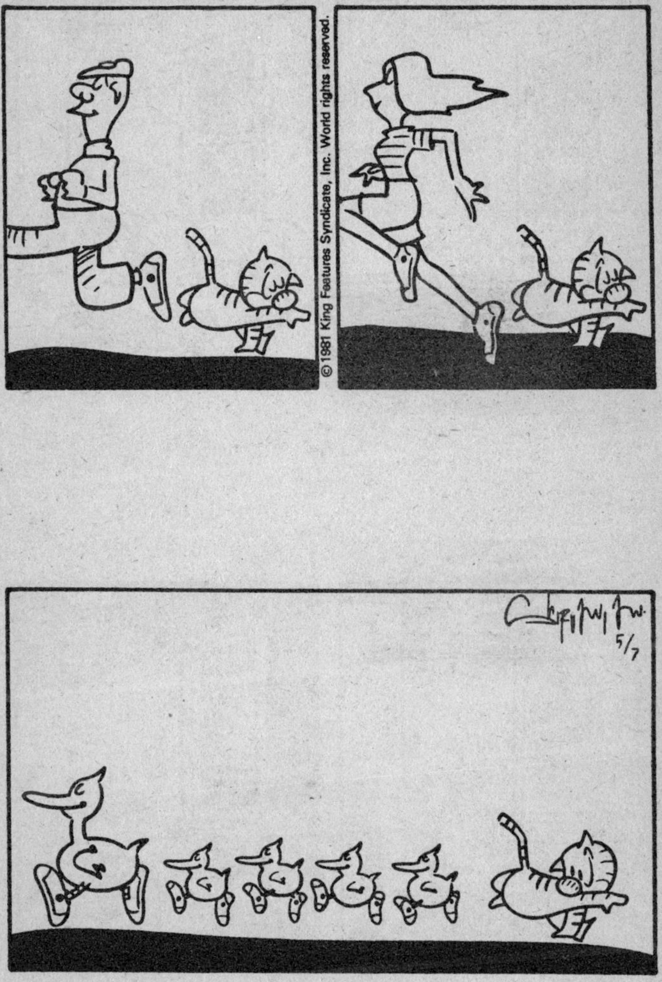
© 1981 King Features Syndicate, Inc. World rights reserved.

BRIMSTONE
© 1981 King Features Syndicate, Inc. World rights reserved.
YAWN!
BRIMSTONE
CLICK!
1-20
BRIMSTONE
Z Z Z
BRIMSTONE

FWEEEEEE!
7/21
© 1981 King Features Syndicate, Inc. World rights reserved.

© 1981 King Features Syndicate, Inc. World rights reserved.
HEE HEE HOO HOO
WHEEZE GASP
HEE HOO
HOME, JAMES— I'M IN NO CONDITION TO WALK!
9/29

MEN AT WORK
©1981 King Features Syndicate, Inc. World rights reserved.
THAT BALL OF STRING DIDN'T WANT TO PLAY
12/19

© 1981 King Features Syndicate, Inc. World rights reserved.
STORE ROOM
BRIMSTONE

Z
Z
Z
Z
WHEW!
STORE ROOM
BRIMSTONE
9/3

SWOOP!
YAWN!
SNATCH
BRIMSTONE
BRIMSTONE
©1981 King Features Syndicate, Inc. World rights reserved.
3/26
BRIMSTONE
SWOOP
CLANG!
BRIMSTONE

© 1981 King Features Syndicate, Inc. World rights reserved.
BRIMSTONE
YECH!

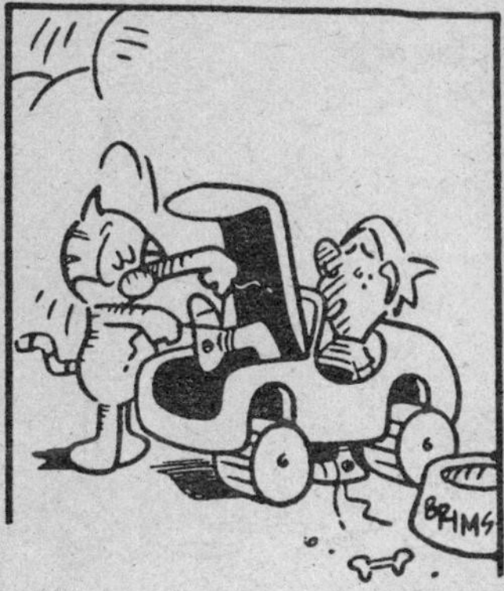
BRIMS

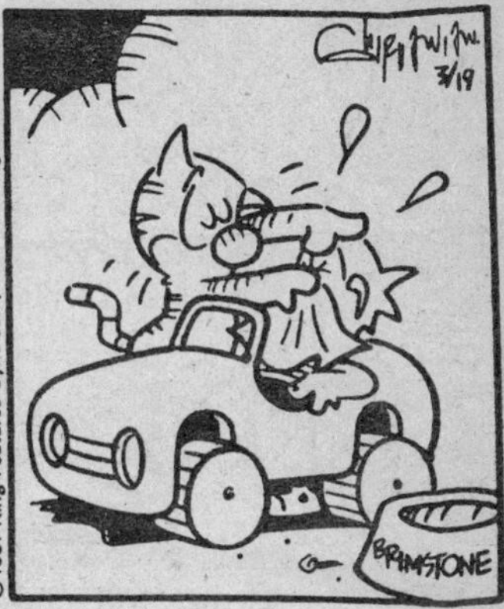
3/19
BRIMSTONE

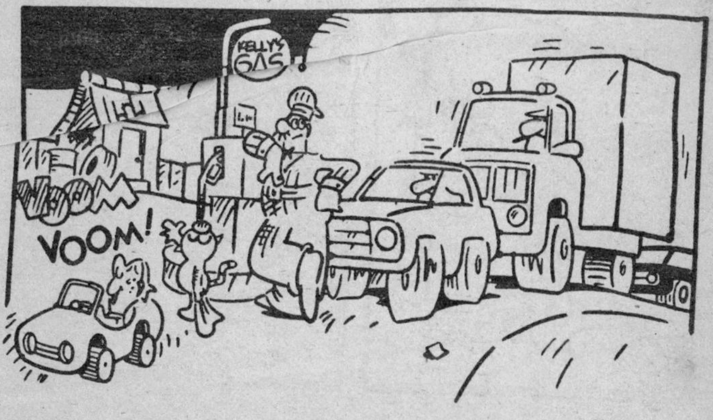
KELLY'S GAS
VOOM!

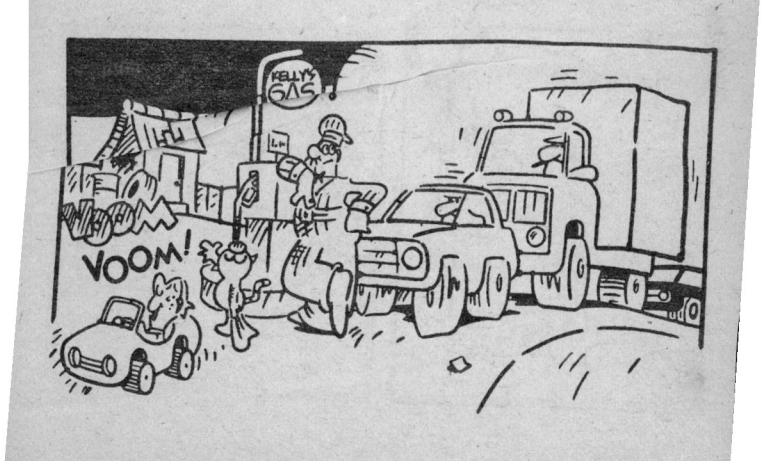

8 A.M.
DUTY
CALL
KELLY'S
GAS
1-29
© 1981 King Features Syndicate, Inc. World rights reserved.
Z
Z
Z
BRIMSTONE

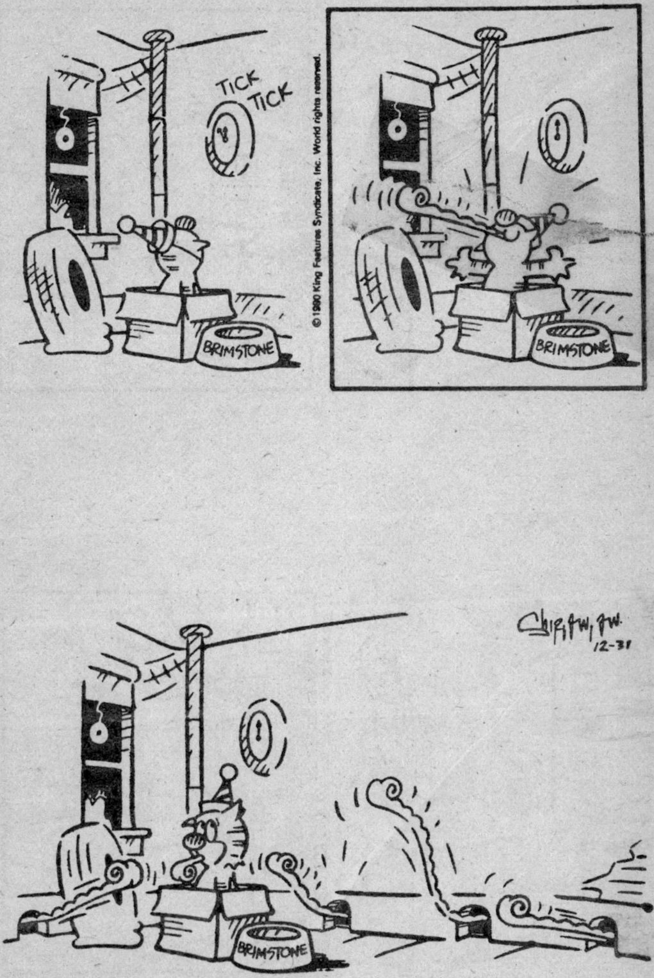
TICK
TICK
BRIMSTONE
BRIMSTONE
BRIMSTONE
12-31

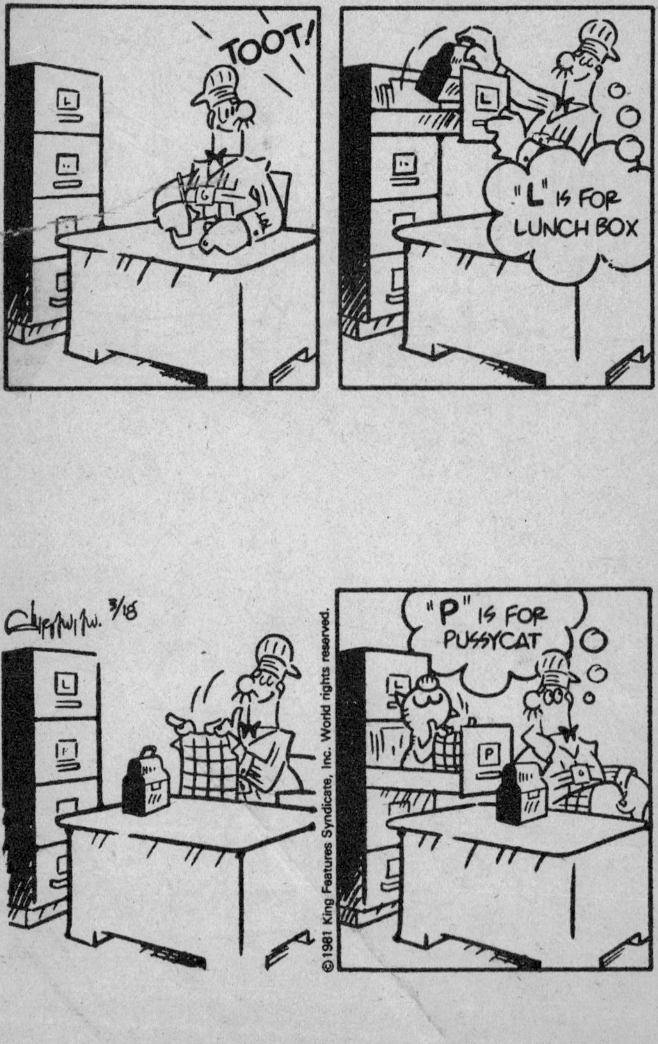
TOOT!
"L" IS FOR LUNCH BOX
3/18
"P" IS FOR PUSSYCAT

ATCHOO!
BRIMSTONE
© 1981 King Features Syndicate, Inc. World rights reserved.
BRIMSTONE
2/13
ATCHOO!
ATCHOO!
ATCHOO!
ATCHOO!
BRIMSTONE

CAT FOOD
TINKLE!
TINKLE!
PLINK!
BRIMSTONE
PLUNK!
©1981 King Features Syndicate, Inc. World rights reserved.

I WISH THEY MADE QUIETER CAT FOOD!
BRIMSTONE
8/27

KELLY'S GAS
MOTOR OIL
BRIMS
© 1981 King Features Syndicate, Inc. World rights reserved.
MOTOR OIL
BRIMS
AUTO-GRAPHS
BRIMSTONE
3/11
KELLY'S GAS

Z
Z
Z
BRI
GARBAGE DISPOSAL
WHIR
CLANK
GRIND!
BRIMS
3/12
BRIMSTONE
MUNCH
SMACK
SLURP
BRIMSTONE

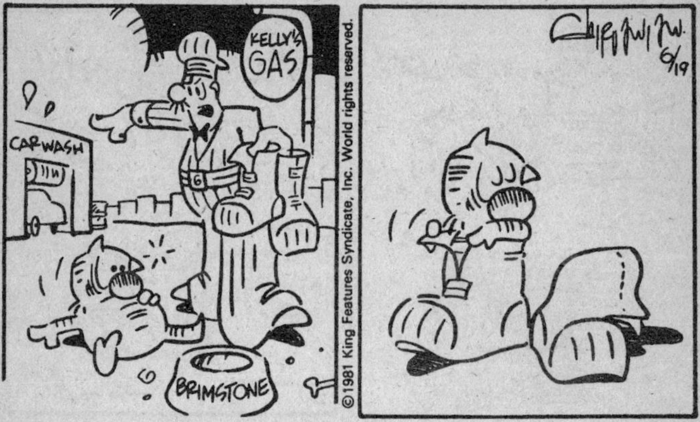
CAR WASH
KELLY'S GAS
BRIMSTONE
6/19

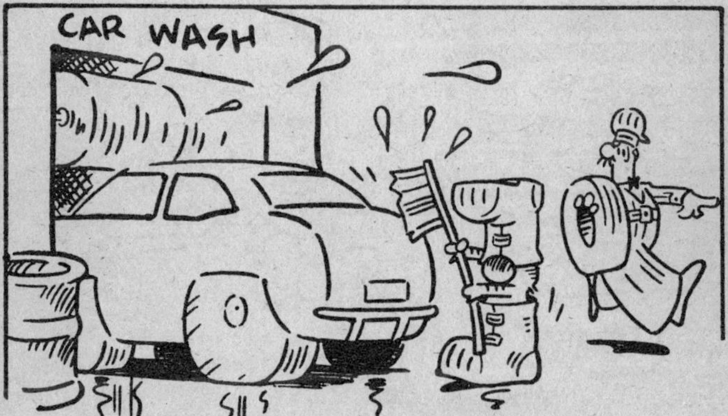
CAR WASH

KELLY'S GAS
SMACK!
BRI
BONK!
PUR-R-R-R
B

3/10
KELLY'S GAS
BONK!
BONK!
BRIMSTONE

BONG! BONG! BONG! BONG! BONG! BONG! BONG! BONG! BONG! BONG! BONG! BONG!
© 1981 King Features Syndicate, Inc. World rights reserved.
6/13
GROWL! GROWL! GROWL! GROWL! GROWL! GROWL! GROWL! GROWL! GROWL! GROWL! GROWL! GROWL!

STORE ROOM
LUNCH TIME!
LUNCH TIME!
BRIMSTONE

©1981 King Features Syndicate, Inc. World rights reserved.
6/1
THIS IS NOT WHAT I HAD IN MIND!

MUNCH!
MUNCH!
BRIMSTONE
©1981 King Features Syndicate, Inc. World rights reserved.
BRIMSTONE

5/30
LEFTOVERS DON'T LAST LONG AROUND HERE
BRIMSTON

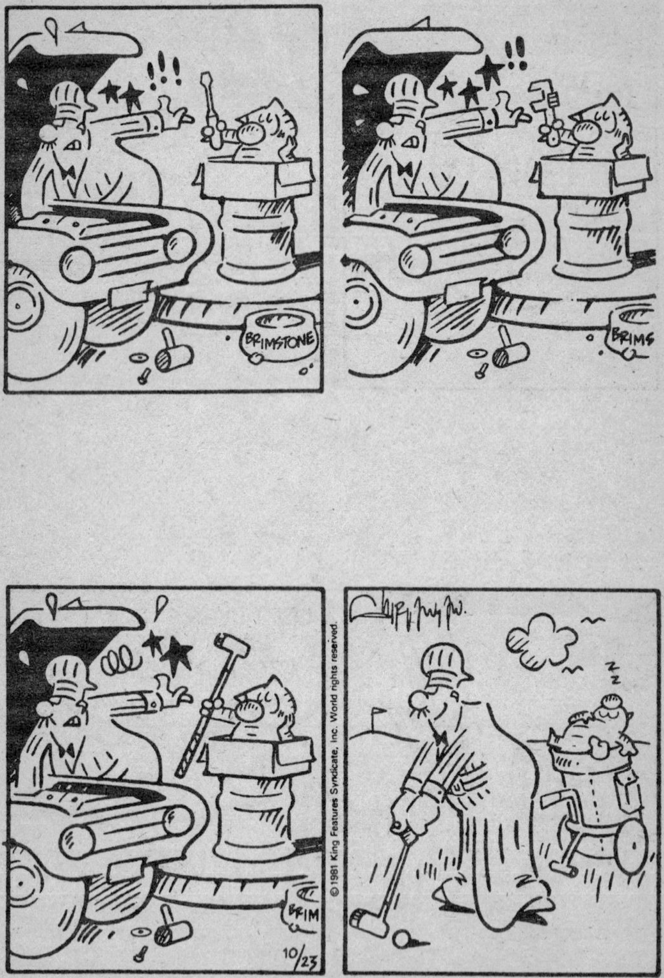
!!!
BRIMSTONE
!!
BRIMS
BRIM
10/23

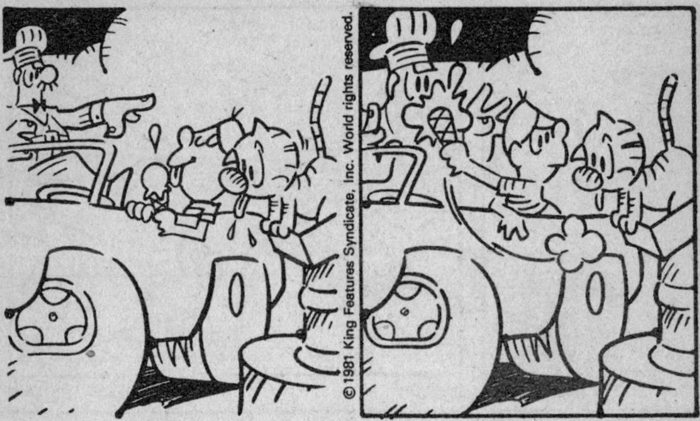

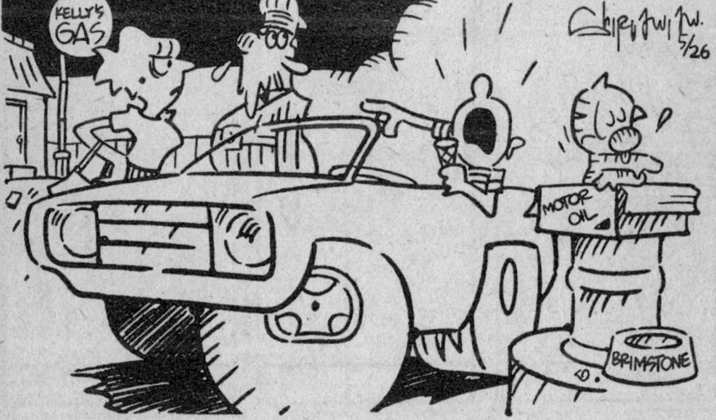
KELLY'S GAS
MOTOR OIL
BRIMSTONE

© 1981 King Features Syndicate, Inc. World rights reserved.
5/18

SCRATCH SCRATCH!
5/20
©1981 King Features Syndicate, Inc. World rights reserved.

PURRRR!
BRIMSTONE
DARN! MY PURRING MECHANISM IS STUCK!
PURRR!
BRIMSTONE

10/24
OH, WELL...
PURRRRR!
BRIMSTONE
BETTER TO BE STUCK IN THE ON POSITION THAN THE OFF!
PURRRR!
BRIMSTONE

INTERESTING LOOKING LITTLE HOLLOW
CONFORMS NICELY TO MY SPECIFI- CATIONS

IT'S FOR SALE? HOW MUCH ARE YOU ASKING FOR IT?
I CAN LIVE WITHOUT IT!
FOR SALE
© 1981 King Features Syndicate, Inc. World rights reserved.

PET PET!
PURRR!

CLICK!
11/12
I THINK I JUST MADE THE COVER OF COSMOPOLITAN

THERE HE IS AGAIN!
MISSED!
SOME DAY I'M REALLY GONNA NAIL YOU!
BUT FOR NOW, LET'S BE FRIENDS
1/18

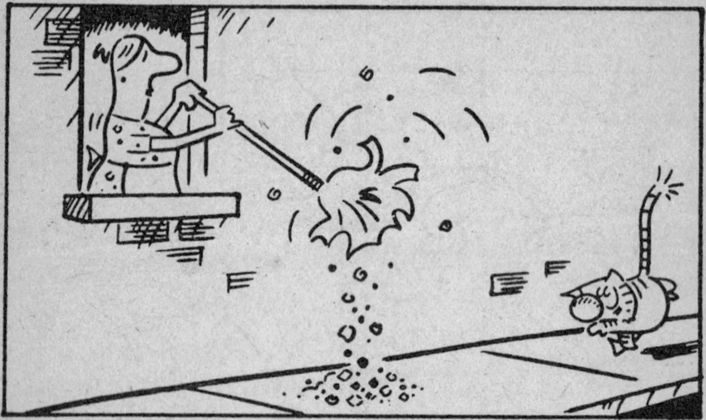

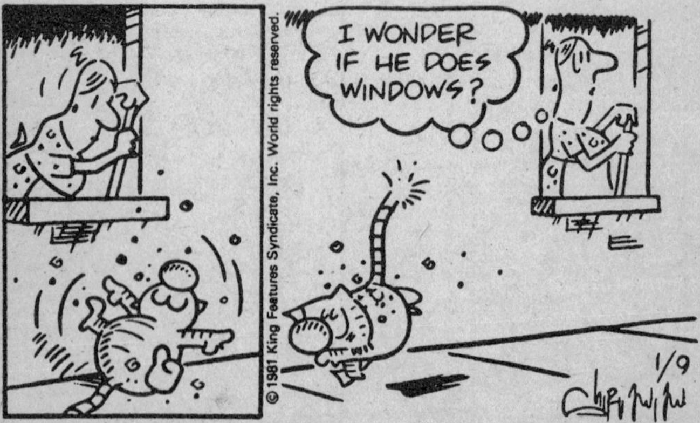

I WONDER IF HE DOES WINDOWS?
1/9

THIS LOOKS LIKE AN INTERESTING RECIPE
COOK BOOK
A PINCH OF OREGANO
PARSLEY FLAKES, SALT, PEPPER

A HALF CUP OF FLOUR, AND A DASH OF NUTMEG
ROLL! ROLL!
NOT BAD— MAYBE A TOUCH MORE PARSLEY

I LOVE HORROR MOVIES
HERE COMES THE MONSTER! THE GIRL OPENS THE DOOR...
GOOSE-BUMP TIME!
EEK!
BRIMSTONE
12/2

PEOPLE THINK IT'S CLEVER OF CATS TO SCRATCH AT THE DOOR TO BE LET IN
SCRATCH SCRATCH
BRIMSTONE

IF THEY'D ONLY LOWER THE DOOR KNOBS I'D HAVE MY OWN SET OF KEYS MADE
BRIMSTONE
1/27

© 1980 King Features Syndicate, Inc. World rights reserved.
12-10
BRIMSTONE

10/22
HEE HEE HOO HOO
HEY! WAS THAT A HAND OR A FOOT?
THE NERVE OF SOME PEOPLE!

KELLY'S GAS
REGULAR
SUPER
UNLEADED
MOTOR OIL
BRIMSTONE
© 1981 King Features Syndicate, Inc. World rights reserved.

KELLY'S GAS
10/1
UNLEADED
UNATTACHED
BRIMSTONE

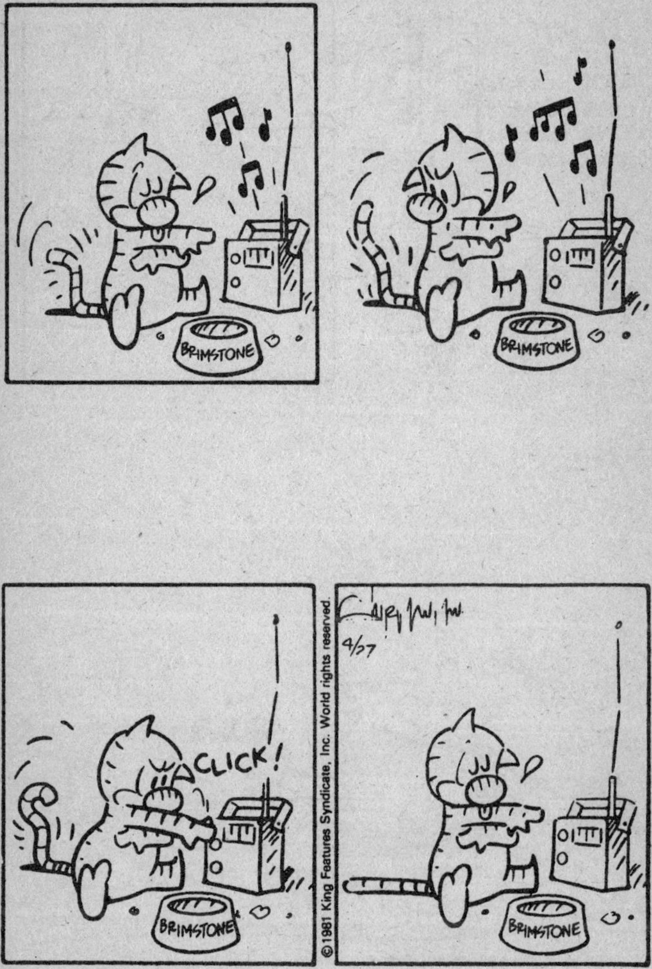
BRIMSTONE
BRIMSTONE
CLICK!
BRIMSTONE
4/27
BRIMSTONE

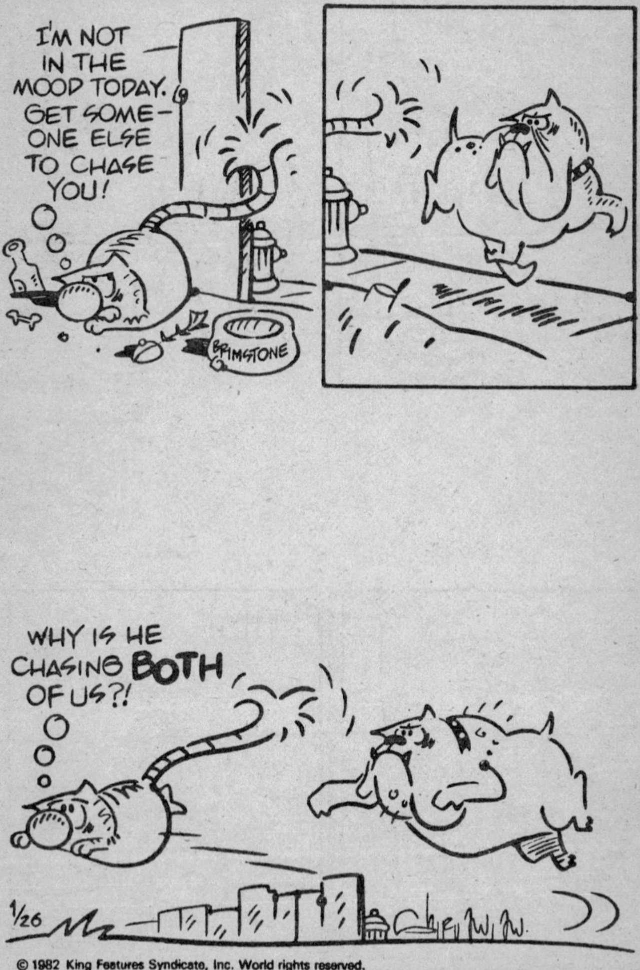
I'M NOT IN THE MOOD TODAY. GET SOME-ONE ELSE TO CHASE YOU!
BRIMSTONE
WHY IS HE CHASING **BOTH** OF US?!
1/26

TICKEE TICKEE
BRIMSTONE
© 1981 King Features Syndicate, Inc. World rights reserved.
PUR-R-R-R!
BONK!

MORNING
HERO CAT NABS CROOK
KELLY'S GAS
4/29

BEG FOR IT!
©1981 King Features Syndicate, Inc. World rights reserved.
10/3
CLIMB CLIMB
MUNCH!
IT WASN'T WORTH BEGGING FOR!
SMACK!

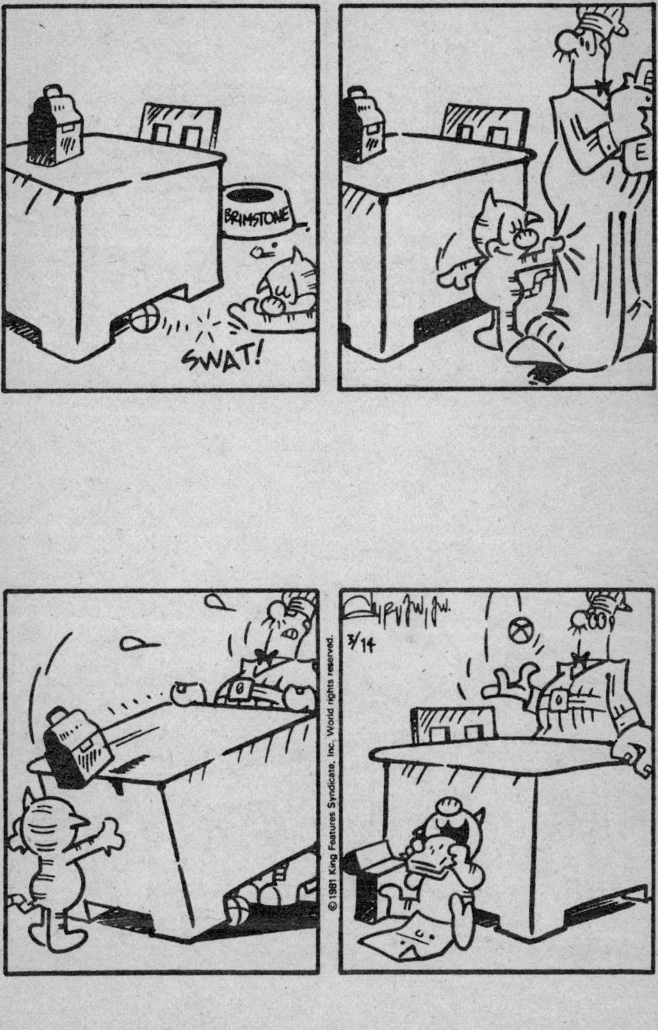
BRIMSTONE
SWAT!
3/14

ROWF! ROWF!
KELLY'S GAS
MOTOR OIL
BRIMSTONE
Z-Z-T!
MOTOR OIL
BRIM
MOTOR OIL
BR
3/16
MOTOR OIL
BR

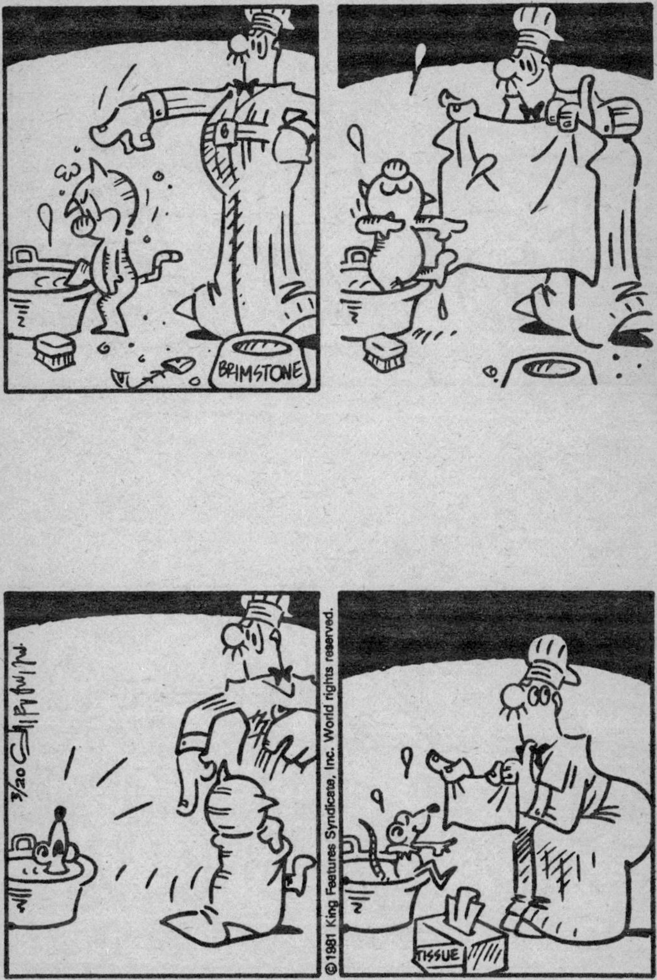
BRIMSTONE
3/20
TISSUE

ROWF!
ROWF!
ROWF!
ROWF!
ROWF!
ROWF!
KELLY'S GAS
MOTOR OIL
BRIMSTONE
5/12

KELLY'S GAS
CAT GOT YOUR TONGUE?
MOTOR OIL
BRIMSTONE

BRIMSTONE
© 1981 King Features Syndicate, Inc. World rights reserved.
LICK!
BRIMSTONE
6/5
BRIMSTONE
SOME LETTER WRITER I AM! I ATE THE STAMP!

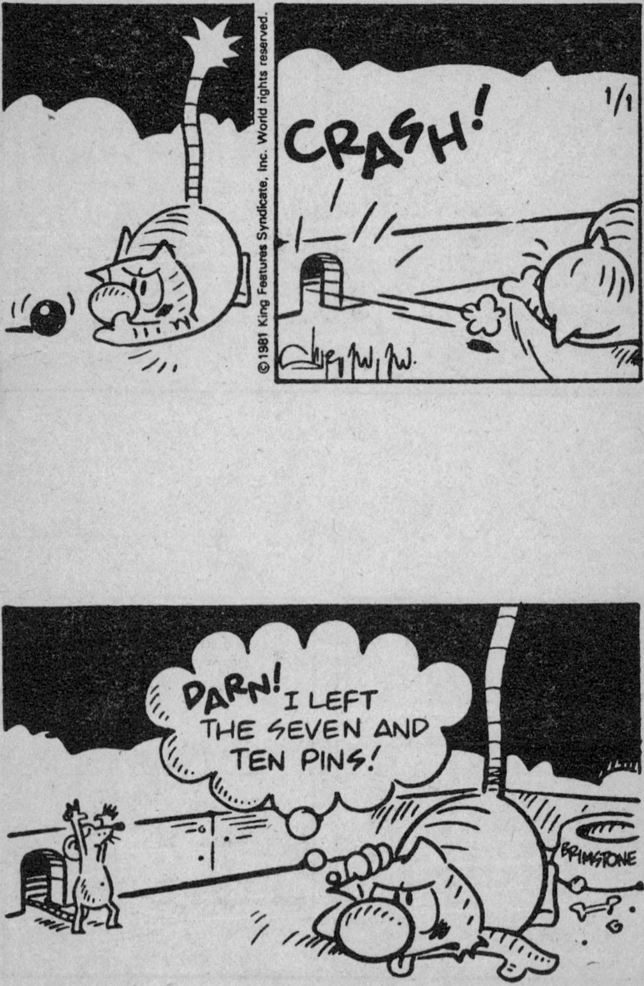
CRASH!
1/1
DARN! I LEFT THE SEVEN AND TEN PINS!
BRIMSTONE

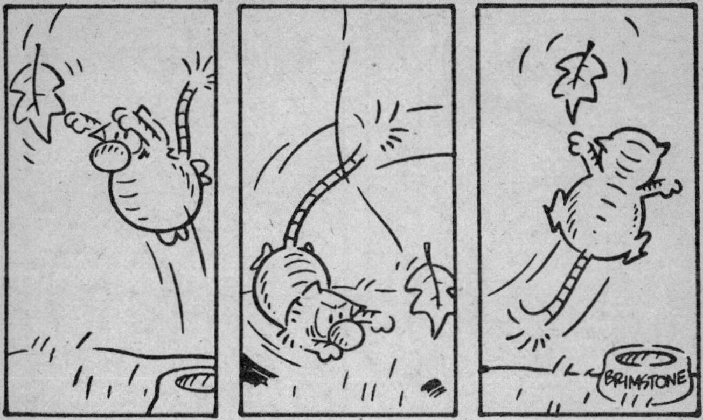
BRIMSTONE

10/27
©1981 King Features Syndicate, Inc. World rights reserved.
HERE WE GO AGAIN!

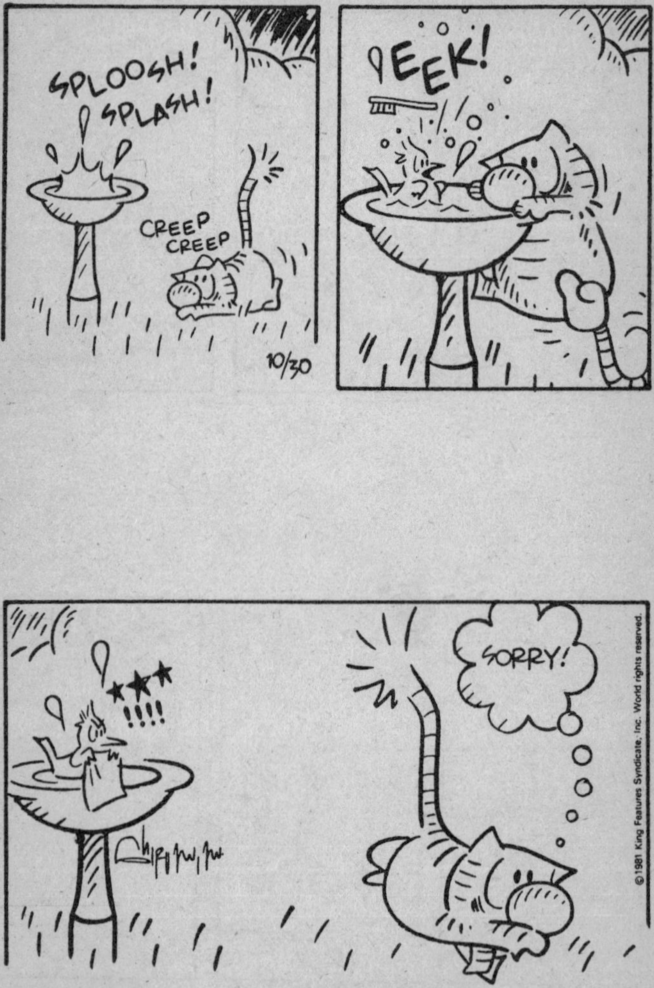
SPLOOSH! SPLASH!
CREEP CREEP
10/30
EEK!
SORRY!